Coconut Mon

by **LINDA MILSTEIN**
pictures by **CHERYL MUNRO TAYLOR**

MACMILLAN
CARIBBEAN

First published 1995 by
WILLIAM MORROW

This edition published 1998 by
MACMILLAN EDUCATION LTD
London and Basingstoke
Companies and representatives throughout the world

ISBN-13: 978-0-333-72708-9
ISBN-10: 0-333-72708-8

10   9   8   7   6   5   4   3   2
07   06

This book is printed on paper suitable for recycling and
made from fully managed and sustained forest sources.

Printed in China

A catalogue record for this book is available from the
British Library.

For Rachel and Samantha Rode,
Kimberly Farber,
Andy and Danny Breiner,
Jaclyn, Samantha, and Noah Adelsberg,
and Noah and Zena Milstein

L.M.

For Brooksie

C. M.T.

CO-CO-NUTS!

One dollar buys a coconut!

Come get your coconuts from the Coconut Mon!

Eight de-LIC-i-ous

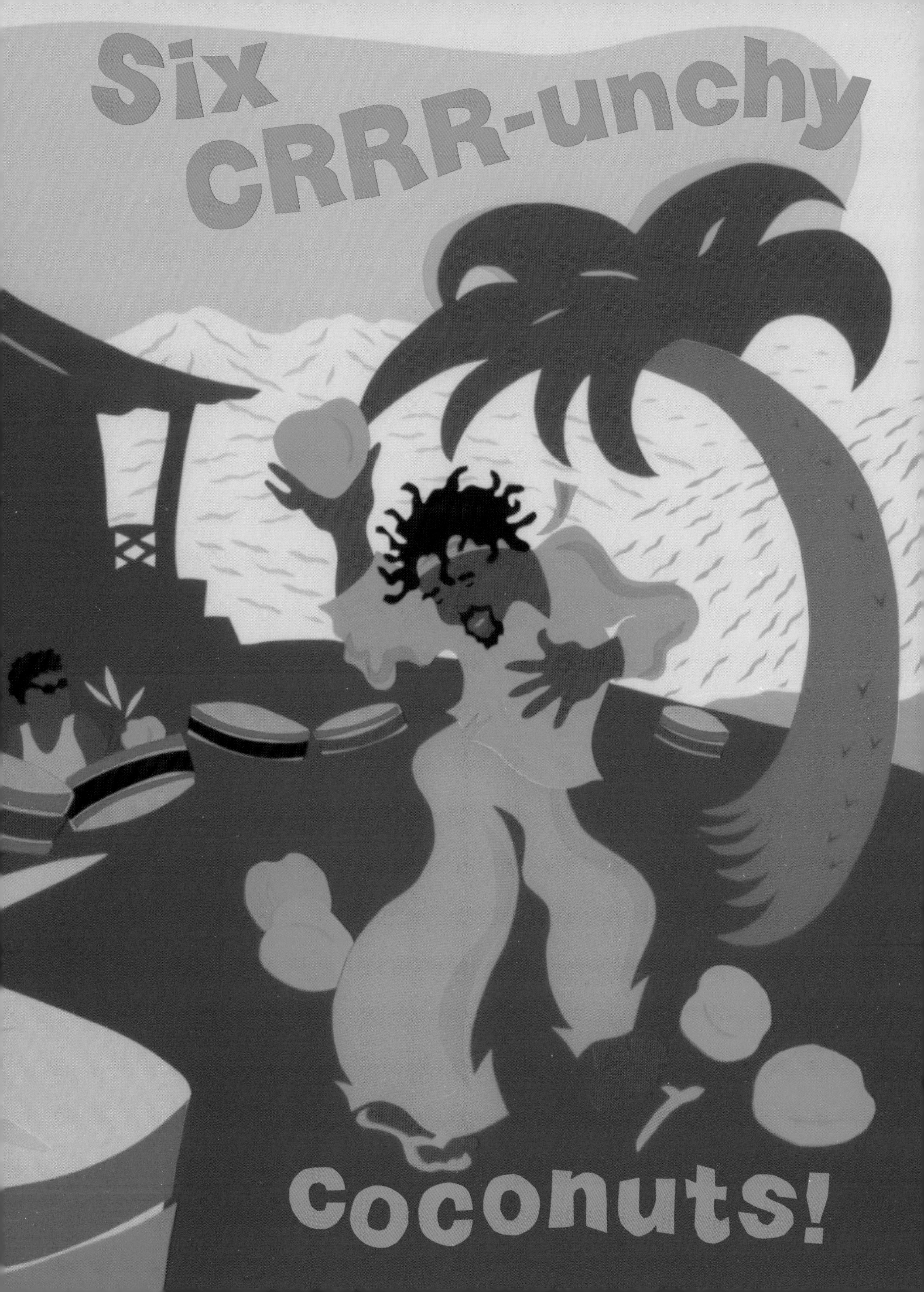
Six
CRRR-unchy
Coconuts!

Coconuts!

Get them from the Coconut Mon!

Four CRRR-isp coconuts!

Three TAAA-sty coconuts!

Two SSSS-weet coconuts!

Get them from the Coconut Mon!

The
very LAST
coconut!

Do you like sweet coconut to eat, young mon?

**Take this coconut!
This GOOOOD coconut!**

Thank you for
this CO-co-nut,
Mr. Coconut Mon.

CO-CO-NUT! De-LIC-i-ous coconut!

Come share
my coconut
EV-ER-Y-ONE!

Enough for all
in the hot, HOT sun!